North Stonington
Christian Academy

Donald Bell
Memorial
1965 - 1983

McGraw-Hill
Children's Publishing

A Division of The **McGraw·Hill** Companies

This edition published in the United States of America in 2003 by
McGraw-Hill Children's Publishing, a division of The McGraw-Hill
Companies.

Send all inquiries to:
McGraw-Hill Children's Publishing
8787 Orion Place
Columbus, OH 43240-4027

www.MHkids.com

Printed in China.

1-56189-309-9

Library of Congress Cataloging-in-Publication Data
on file with the publisher.

1 2 3 4 5 6 7 8 9 BRI 07 06 05 04 03 02

First published in Great Britain in 2002 by Brimax
An imprint of Octopus Publishing Group Ltd
2-4 Heron Quays, London E14 4JP

© 1997 bohem press, Zurich, Switzerland

"I'm going to the North Pole to find Santa Claus," Peter told his friends. "He dropped his hat, and I'm going to give it back to him."

"You can't see Santa Claus," said his friends. "He comes while we are sleeping. Only grownups are allowed to see him."

Like all little polar bears, Peter believed he was much bigger than he was. "But I am grown up now," he said. And with that, he set off for the North Pole.

Peter walked through the snow all day. When he finally reached the North Pole, he found the strangest thing. An old woman was knitting a red hat, just like the one he had found. And she was doing it in right in the middle of the North Pole.

"Hello," said the old woman. "I see you found one of my hats."

"Your hat?" said Peter. "I thought it was Santa's hat."

"It is," she said. "Have a seat and I'll explain."

"Every year," she said, "while Santa is busy wrapping presents, I knit him lots of new hats. Sometimes I throw one up in the air and let the wind carry it away. If a child finds a hat, it reminds him that Christmas is on its way."

"Like this." She tossed two hats into the air. They swirled and danced away on the breeze.

The old woman gave Peter a cup of hot chocolate and some cookies.

"Please, may I stay and wait for Santa Claus?" asked Peter.

"I'm afraid not," the old woman answered. "Only grownups can see Santa Claus. You must go home and go to sleep. Then Santa Claus will come."

Peter headed home, very disappointed. Couldn't she see what a big bear he was? He just couldn't believe he wouldn't get to see Santa Claus after coming all this way!

Suddenly, Peter heard a jingling noise behind him. He turned around and couldn't believe what he saw—lots of men dressed in red!

Who are those men? Peter wondered. He hurried back toward them. When he got close, he could see there were hundreds of Santa Clauses, all dressed exactly alike, all loading presents onto their sleighs. *One of them had to be the real Santa,* Peter thought, *but which one could it be?*

When the old woman saw that Peter had returned, she
exclaimed, "You're still here. I thought you were going home to
sleep just like the other little polar bears!"

"I'm not little," said Peter. "I'm big enough to meet Santa."

Just then, a strong wind whooshed across the snow. It smelled like gumdrops and candy canes.

The old woman smiled. "This is the Christmas wind," she said. "Sometimes, when it's strong enough, it will show you something special."

The wind blew stronger and stronger. Peter closed his eyes and dug his claws into the snow.

Presents blew from the sleds, and the Santas rushed around to pick them up.

And Peter, who really *was* a little bear, felt himself lift off the ground. An icy gust tossed him high into the sky.

As Peter swirled round and round, he looked down upon the North Pole. All of the Santa Clauses stood far, far below him. Peter watched in amazement as the Santas formed the shape of one big Santa Claus.

Then Peter understood what the Christmas wind was showing him. Santa Claus could not possibly deliver presents all over the world by himself in just one night. He needed help. These men dressed as Santa must be his helpers.

The wind began to die down. Peter closed his eyes as he drifted slowly toward the ground.

Plop! He landed headfirst in the snow.

"What did you see?" asked the old woman.

Peter told her about the shape the Santas had formed in the snow.

The old woman smiled at Peter. "Now you know the secret of the North Pole," she said. "And it is time for us to go. Santa Claus has lots of children to visit tonight. And you must get home to bed."

Before Peter left, the old woman gave him a brightly wrapped present. "I know you didn't get to meet Santa Claus," she said, "but this should make you feel better."

Peter thanked her for all her kindness and waved goodbye.

When he got home, Peter opened his gift. It was one of Santa Claus's hats! The label on the hat said, "For one of Santa's helpers." Peter was so pleased that he put it on right away. Then he noticed a message in the box.

The message read:

> *Here's a Santa hat to wear*
> *For an almost grownup bear.*
> *Put it on and then you'll be*
> *A special helping friend to me.*
>
> Santa

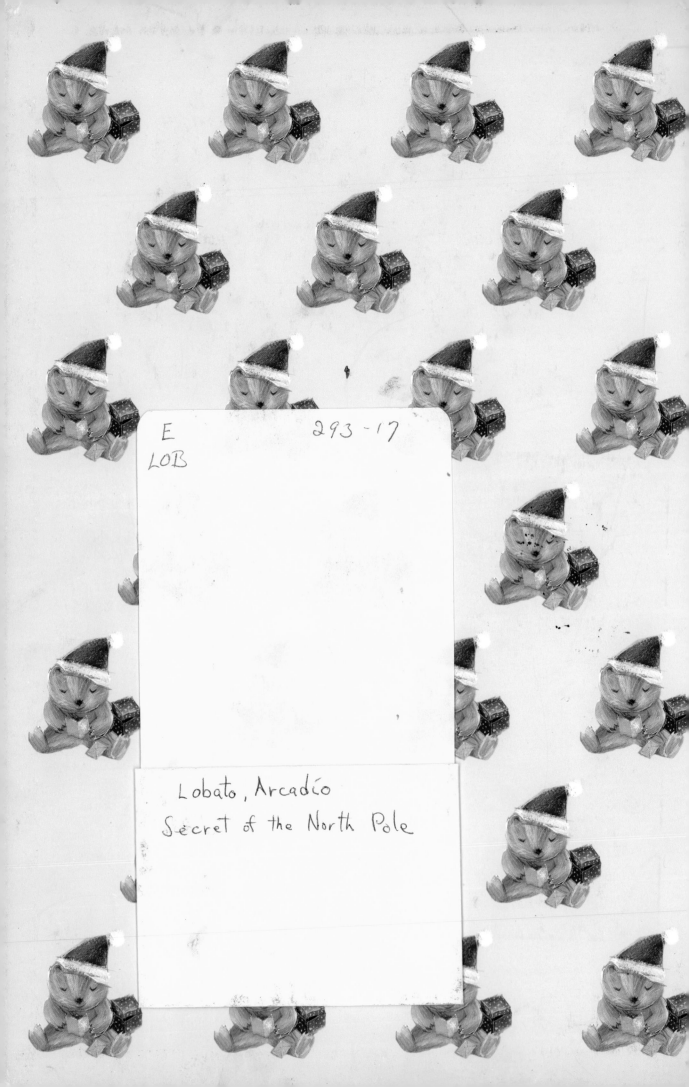